ADVANCE PRAISE

"It's not often I get that viscerally emotional on behalf of a fictional character. In a setting of overt fantasy, Angélique Jamail has created some of the most real people I've encountered via text in a long time."

—Ari Marmell
Hot Lead, Cold Iron, and The *Widdershins* Series

"A silver vein of irony runs through . . . It is a witty tale of conformity, prejudice, and transformation, in a world that is disturbing as much for its familiarity as for its strangeness. In a place where everyone is different, Elsa is the wrong kind of different, and that means facing pity, discrimination, danger, and sharp teeth. Dive into this story, readers, and confront them for yourself; it may just change the way you feel about things . . ."

—Marie Marshall
The Everywhen Angels and *I am not a fish*

"Jamail takes a classic story and puts a fresh and unique twist on it . . . She writes in a very straightforward prose, which when peppered with the magical realism . . . creates an interesting juxtaposition of styles. I most appreciate how real some of these characters are, and I was amazed at how Jamail played with my emotions with such a brief story. I eagerly await the next installment!"

—Reader review

"The writing itself is magical. [For] anyone who enjoys magical realism or anyone who just enjoys sparklingly original pieces that are poetic and truly well-written."

—Reader review

"A lovely coming-of-age story about a young woman who is struggling to realize who she is meant to be. It captures the struggle many post-college graduates face trying to find a career they'll be happy in, but with a beautiful supernatural allegory. Jamail paints a fascinating world, and I look forward to reading more books of hers!"

—Reader review

"Jamail's prose is vivid and precise, and the implications of this magical world resonate far beyond a seemingly simple story. Transformation, after all, is the stuff of fairy tales, of fantasy literature from its very beginnings (like the wild man Enkidu from Gilgamesh). Elsa's seemingly simple story shimmers with allegorical possibilities. How interesting that the truest manifestation of a 'self' is to exhibit animal features . . . It leads one—or at least this reader—to reconsider the ways we think about and construct the self, the ways we value and talk about self-realization or self-respect, and to reflect on the ways that it is seemingly both rooted in human and animal nature to fear and distrust difference. What looks like a simple, engaging story on the surface here has profound depths."

—Reader review

"I loved this book! It is so imaginative and beautifully written! With its quirky imagery and mystical aura, it is a most unusual story with something to say about the perils of growing up in a society that encourages conformity. A most unusual read!"

"You know how some people remind you of, or even resemble animals? In the world Jamail creates in this short but intense and fully-imagined novella, people are part-animal, or at least manifest Animal Affinities that are taken to be not just signs of their maturation into adults but also the fullest realization of selfhood . . . At once a powerful allegory about difference and a charming story about self-realization, Jamail's book satisfies on several levels and renders up such vivid imagery that the reader isn't quite prepared to leave that world behind, even when the story reaches its satisfying end."

A
NARROWING
PATH

A
NARROWING
PATH

ANGÉLIQUE JAMAIL

MEMENTO VIVERE PRESS

A Narrowing Path © 2025
MEMENTO VIVERE PRESS LLC
Printed in the United States

Published by **MEMENTO VIVERE PRESS**
www.mementoviverepress.com
First Edition, May 2025

Publisher, Ynes Freeman
ynes@mementoviverepress.com

Editor-in-Chief and Formatter, Leo Otherland
leo@mementoviverepress.com

Cover art and design by Maria Spada
www.mariaspada.com

Publisher's Cataloging-in-Publication Data
Names: Jamail, Angélique.
Title: A narrowing path / Angélique Jamail.
Description: Green Bay, WI : Memento Vivere
    Press, 2025.
Identifiers: LCCN 2025935462 | ISBN
    9781964501048 (pbk.) | ISBN
    9781964501055 (ebook)
Subjects: LCSH: Human-animal relationships –
    Fiction. | Genetic transformation – Fiction.
    | Conformity – Fiction. | LCGFT: Magic
    realist fiction. | Fantasy fiction. | BISAC:
    FICTION / Magical Realism. | FICTION /
    Fantasy / Contemporary. | FICTION /
    Women.
Classification: LCC PS3610.A43 2025 | DDC 813
J--dc23
LC record available at
https://lccn.loc.gov/2025935462

DEDICATION

for Andy, Emma, Justin, Meredith, Rachel, Sean, Stacey,
and Vali
and so many others
because cousins are so important

Author's Note

This story contains elements that may be troubling to some readers, including an unloving family dynamic and one character's attempt to unalive herself. The reasons that people sometimes make such a decision often stem from a mistaken belief that there is no other solution to their problems, sometimes because they cannot see the full picture of their lives in all its mysterious wonder.

If you or someone you know is suffering, there are ways beyond it. The path is truly less narrow that it sometimes seems.

Suicide Prevention Hotline
- call 988 for Lifeline or 1-800-273-TALK (8255)

National Resources for Mental Health Treatment and Referrals
- call 1-800-662-HELP (4357)
- text your zip code to 435748 (HELP4U)

Please proceed in the way that will best allow for your own self-care and well-being.

With love,
Angélique

1

ELSA'S PARENTS and sister have become meaner than usual, and her cat, Jonas, resents her. She has a nagging concern he wants to eat her.

"He bit me again this morning—I woke up to find half the toes on my left foot in his mouth! I kicked him away, but he just came back, all fangs and hissing, till I locked him in the coat closet."

But that's only the beginning, Elsa tries to explain to her cousin Gerard. She has to speak in short bursts: he's conducting his water exercises, his head bobbing in and out of the water in orderly arcs. She knew she'd be interrupting his routine, but this morning's episode has brought things to a head. On her way to work, anxiety commandeered her every thought and movement. Before she could catch her breath, she found herself tearing through Gerard's garden gate and rushing to his salt-water pool.

"Oh, Elsa," he says, his feet spiraling around a large stalk of kelp just below the water's surface. He runs a watery hand across his spiky brown hair, and brine curls down his back. "What are you going to do?"

"What's even worse, my landlord left another threat-of-eviction notice today." She sets her briefcase down near a baby potted corpse flower and ventures closer to the pool. "I've done nothing wrong. My rent is always on time. I'm a quiet, orderly tenant. I thought getting a cat would mollify the building association, but unless I *become* a cat, I don't think it'll help."

Gerard dunks, flips neatly into a ball, and spins back up; he swims to where she stands at the edge of the pool and rises. "Have you had any hints of your self?" He looks at her carefully, scrutinizing, and she wants to shrink into the empty void of mediocrity. Still, his voice is tender. "Anything at all?"

"No," she murmurs, mesmerized by the ripples his body makes, the way the water slaps against the side of the pool and then laps backward over itself, folding the brine under to dissolve in a never-ending cycle of thrash and renewal.

"I'm not sure I approve of where you're living, anyway. Those awful gangs—I read about them in the newspaper. Packs attacking Plain Ones right and left, even children."

"I saw that, too." She doesn't mention that one of those miscreant dogs last night took a sledgehammer to her mailbox, busted it into a dozen shards, or that she saw his companion breaking raw eggs on her car's back windshield. She watched through the slats of her window blinds, and then was too afraid to go back out in the dark to clean the eggs off. "They usually go for adults, though—people who ought to have spread their wings by now." Her shame for the disgrace she's caused her family burns on her face.

Gerard smiles. "Come in for a swim. You'll feel better." He shoots backward through the water, darkened spiny ridges flashing on his skin.

If only it were as easy as he makes it sound. She almost wants to jump in—she wishes she could—but then imagines how painful it would be. "I can't," she says. She makes an excuse. "Work."

"Of course. The monster."

"I've never been a swimmer, anyway." Even standing for too long in the shower makes her skin feel prickly and sore; she usually just soaps up before turning the water on and then washes her hair in the sink. "I think I'm allergic to water."

He laughs. "Off you go, then. See you later—"
His words bubble as he dives backward.

Elsa trudges out the gate, hardly even waving
back at the friendly teenage centaur, in the exuberant
flush of early transformation, mowing the lawn next
door.

2

ELSA HEARS the snarling from all the way downstairs and pushes the six button again, as if that would make the elevator go any faster. She doesn't want to be late. As the doors finally, slowly open, she rushes out, bumping her shoulder on the metal edge of one of them. An accountant from the third floor, his mottled brown and gray hair in disarray, crashes into her as he flies toward the exit.

"I'm so sorry," she says, helping him collect his fallen papers. Quietly she asks, "Are you all right?"

He pushes his round, dark-rimmed glasses farther up his beaky nose. "Those two new secretaries missed a staff meeting last night."

He doesn't have to say any more about the displeasure of the monster behind the big oak desk.

Elsa adjusts the neat hair clip she always wears and steps cautiously into the sixth floor receiving area, unwilling to navigate the labyrinth of low-walled cubicles to her own workstation next to the monster's room.

Even from here she can see fresh piles of beige folders on her desk, but horrible sounds are coming from the boss's office. She realizes with chagrin her briefcase is still on Gerard's patio and panics, turns quickly around, and walks back out to the elevator bank. Artwork on the walls and a large aquarium filled with colorful fish and other placid creatures calm her. One young man from her office, a new hire, is staring mindlessly at a large, abstract photograph as if trying to lose himself in it. Another employee rushes out to stare at a particularly soothing canvas of gray paint.

She presses her fingertips to the front of the aquarium and several fish swim up to her. The larger ones seem to smile; the smaller ones seem to be trying to suck her fingertips through the glass. Watching the kelp and anemone and angelfish tranquilizes Elsa's nerves enough for her to go back inside. She turns around.

Lois, the switchboard operator, quietly beckons her. Thick glasses usually cover her pretty orange eyes, but today the spectacles sit atop her head, holding back a curly mane of dark copper hair that looks mussed, as if from dodging projectiles. She doesn't look frightened, though, despite the palpable fear among the rest of the staff. Elsa hurries over.

"Are the secretaries going to be fired?" she asks. Three empty coffee cups clutter Lois's desk, and dirt smudges highlight a dent in the tan wall behind it. The heavy wooden door to the monster's interior office shakes suddenly, as if something the size of a potted tree has just been hurled at it.

"Already done. The question now is whether they'll have to be carried out."

They watch for several tense minutes as the growling and yelling and sounds of people running around and things being thrown continue to distract everyone from working.

Suddenly, a shriek from the interior chamber makes Elsa cringe. She recognizes the voice of that secretary—another Plain One, she's sure, although the woman tried to keep it a secret. But Elsa knew, could see it in the nervous way the woman watched other people interact, in the dejected slump of her shoulders when she thought no one was looking at her.

Elsa debated whether to approach her, whether she would welcome sympathetic company.

Or perhaps they would each make the other more of a pariah, since no one liked it when underdogs banded together. Maybe the secretary would be angry and offended, would keep trying to hide who she wasn't.

Or maybe Elsa was wrong about her and would be rebuffed, her position as outcast further solidified.

She finally decided it was easier not to try to be understood.

There's another crash. It sounds like her inner debate is quickly becoming irrelevant.

A tap on Elsa's shoulder makes her jump. Gerard is standing there, holding out her briefcase.

"Elsa, dear, you need someone to look after you," he says.

"No, I don't," she mutters.

"Who are you?" Lois purrs appreciatively, shaking his slightly webbed hand.

"My cousin Gerard," Elsa says. She holds up the briefcase, annoyed with herself for having forgotten it. "Thanks for bringing this." Grudgingly she adds, "You've saved my hide."

The monster's door opens, and one secretary—not the one who piqued Elsa's curiosity—stumbles quickly out, red hair up like a coxcomb. Her sleeve is gashed open. She points sloppily toward his office and mumbles, "Kelly . . . ambulance."

There's a roar, and Elsa clutches her briefcase to her chest. She can see the horns and hairy shoulders. The boss is nearly seven feet tall.

Lois sighs and picks up the phone on her desk. "I hope he's paid up on the workers' comp policy," she says.

"That supervisor of yours is a nasty customer," Gerard says evenly. "Somewhere in Crete a maze is missing its pet."

Elsa knows she ought to try to find a new job. The monster has too much of a temper, and this sort of thing is happening more often. But she hasn't been on the job market in a long time and doubts there are many opportunities available for people like her.

There's another familiar snarl, the monster clearing his throat. He can't even do that without menace. The underling in the cubicle next to her jumps at the sound.

Elsa will look for job listings this weekend.

3

IT'S ELSA'S mother's birthday, and the whole family has been summoned to dinner at her parents' house, but just being around them all twists Elsa's stomach into knots. After a salade niçoise she couldn't even choke down, Mother announces that Elsa's father has bought her a swimming pool for her birthday; they'll break ground within two weeks. Everyone else is excited. When Elsa doesn't muster the same enthusiasm as the rest of the family, her father asks what her problem is.

"Dad, you know I can't swim—"

"No, you *won't* swim," he grouses. "There's a difference."

This is technically true. Elsa chooses not to submerge herself in vats of acid, too.

"I should've just thrown you into the water when you were little instead of listening to you whine." He harrumphs, a gargoyle hunkering over his dinner. He and Elsa recall her traumatic first experience with a swimming pool in very different ways. "Faced with sink or swim, I'll bet you'd have figured out a way to dog-paddle."

Elsa stares at her plate, pushes the food around on it. She nibbles a little at the bacon wrapping the shrimp and has eaten half her wheat roll, but nothing tastes good.

Her sister, Joan, is there with her husband, Neil, and their eight-month-old son, Stuart. The evening continues in its typical way: Joan and Neil and Stuart are the stars with their gaiety and antics; Elsa greatly vexes her mother (*Why doesn't she ever go out? Why doesn't she ever bring friends over at the holidays? Is she ever going to get married?*), which makes her father grumble, which makes Joan suggest Elsa do something different with her hair or her clothes or go out more or do *some*thing, which makes Neil pay more attention to Stuart, which makes Elsa's mother say how much she loves grandchildren and would like to have more someday while glaring at her younger daughter.

"Sure, Mother, I'll have some grandchildren for you. Right after I sprout two more legs and some wings and become a butterfly."

Everyone becomes quiet then, the family's frustrated dance around the subject of Elsa's Plainness stuttering to a halt. Her mother looks wistful, as if she hopes such a transformation might one day come to pass and doesn't understand why it hasn't.

In the ensuing uncomfortable silence, Elsa surveys them all: her parents, prominent figures in society, their stateliness exuding from every pore even in the privacy of their home; Neil with his raven coloring; Stuart, soft fuzzy hair on his velvet scalp, just like Joan had when she was young. And then Joan. Tall, graceful, even her freckles a lovely blanket over golden skin. Like her mother, a perfect giraffe.

"Elsa, I have the number of a doctor I want you to call," Mother finally says. "One of my friends suggested him."

"I've been to see doctors before," Elsa reminds her. They examined every inch of her, inside and out, subjected her to the most embarrassing questions ever, but could find no evidence of her animal affinity.

The last doctor, a specialist, recommended shock therapy as a way to bring out Elsa's true nature. "Your whole life will improve once we figure out what you've got hiding away inside of you," he said, his small black eyes like beads in his ruddy face. "No one will question your intelligence or competence ever again." He grinned at her with thin lips. "You might even find a boyfriend finally." At Elsa's surprised look, he shrugged. "Your dad told me you can't even get a date. No worries, though. Once we figure out what you are, the whole world will see you in a more favorable light." He cleared his throat and pinched his prescription pad, began scrawling notes. "I recommend eight to ten sessions—"

"Absolutely not!" Elsa said, tugging the medical gown tighter around herself. She wouldn't endure some medievally inspired torture just so her parents could feel better about their unusual kid.

The doctor cast her an indignant look. "Has anything else worked yet? Without an evident affinity, you're only half your self."

Elsa leveled an angry look at him that was more fear than backbone. "I'm not interested in shock therapy, thanks."

"Fine," the doctor replied coolly. "Enjoy being a Plain One." Then he left the exam room, closing the door behind him with a little more force than was strictly necessary. Elsa put her clothes back on and left as quickly as she could. Her parents were annoyed with her for that, too.

"He was one of the best, Elsa," her father snapped. "I had to pull some strings to get you that appointment. He's usually booked seven months in advance."

Elsa still can't decide whether she appreciates her father's efforts, or if he simply wanted to reassure himself it wasn't his fault she's so deficient. Either way, she knows she isn't going back.

Dinner ends with a hedonistic dessert to which Joan politely demurs. "Watching my figure," she says, smiling. As if Joan has to worry about that—she grazes all day and never puts on an ounce. Elsa takes a bite of the mousse cake and finds it delicious. Suddenly she's hungry, but she hasn't eaten three bites before Joan stops her. "Seriously? That'll go straight to your hips."

Later, when Elsa gathers her purse and keys to go home, she glances back at everyone chatting away and realizes no one is noticing her. The family room—a concoction of Stuart's toys and Joan's knitting bag and some books about bird signs Neil brought over for her father to read—is filled with the presence of Joan's family. Nothing of Elsa's anywhere, except for the plain white envelope on the small table by the door. It contains a check, a small monthly supplement because Elsa's income hasn't kept pace with the rising cost of living, so that she can have an apartment of her own.

Nights like this, Elsa just knows her parents wish they'd stopped with the first child.

4

IT TAKES about six months for Elsa's parents' pool to be finished. The deck takes another week, and then her parents arrange a pool party to celebrate the start of summer and their new backyard oasis. Elsa receives an invitation in the mail with her monthly check, a subtle but firm reminder that her attendance is expected.

"They could've just called me," she says to Jonas, showing him the card. He swats at it with his front paw and knocks it out of her hand. Despite her attempts to buy his affection with toys and catnip and, those having failed, a tiny mouse that just made her sick when she had to clean its guts off the floor, their relationship has not improved in the last six months any more than her feelings toward her family have.

In fact, aside from two more new mailboxes, very little in her life has changed, but the time has passed quickly because she's always working. Besides seeing Gerard sometimes, she has no life outside of that horrible job. She hasn't quit, though, since she isn't sure she can find another one. Work opportunities are few and far between for Plain Ones, even those who are educated, as she is. In the five employment applications she started to fill out, the box which was once labeled "Special Skills" now asks for "Animal Affinity." It appears that in a tightening economy, employers can't afford training people who will never reach their full potential, never understand the world in a complex way, never *truly mature*.

The monster has gone through three more secretaries. Elsa and Lois have started eating lunch together once or twice a week in the building's cafeteria, and Elsa finds her laid-back attitude about work soothing, but she isn't any closer to understanding this woman who's like a patch of sunlight in the middle of a corral of scurrying, dismal creatures. She has such a clear-eyed presence, so much confidence. Elsa wonders how old Lois was when her affinity emerged, whether it came on early and how that affected her adolescence and early adulthood. Or whether it came on late and she just persevered—and if so, how. But these are not polite questions.

Elsa rummages through her dresser to find her bathing suit, to try it on before showing up in it at her parents' house. She bought one for sunbathing, but that was ages ago, during a fit of optimism the year after she graduated from college, and who knows if she can still fit into it.

She finally finds it in the back of the bottom drawer: a glaring purple bikini she grimaces at and decides she'll replace even if she *is* still that size. Sure enough, it doesn't come close to fitting properly. The bottom is too tight and no longer covers her. This is no surprise—she knows women get rounder as they get older—but the top doesn't fit anymore, either. Elsa never thought her chest would get any larger. It's always been disappointingly average but now seems to have a certain fullness. The purple top stretches across her breasts obscenely, and she has trouble clasping it shut at the back. Elsa removes the bikini immediately and tosses it into her wastebasket. She takes the clip out of her hair—she can see, even despite the tangles, it has grown so long while she wasn't paying attention—and looks at her naked body in the mirror.

"I've never been curvy before," she says quietly with a cautious smile. She turns to look across the room at Jonas, lying on the bed. "What do you think, kitty? Time for me to go shopping?"

He rolls over onto his back and turns his head to the wall. She walks toward him and rubs his belly just a little, the hopeful overture of peace an extension of her buoyed spirits. He even begins to purr, but then the wail of sirens a few blocks away interrupts the moment. He bites her hand hard enough to draw blood. She recoils in surprise and anger as he licks his chops repeatedly, staring at her.

Scowling, she tells him, "I wasn't planning to take you with me anyway!" Then she drags on an oversize t-shirt and goes to find a bandage.

5

IT OCCURS to Elsa that she can make her own social event if she just insists on reserving the time to do it. At lunch on Friday, she invites Lois over for dinner the next weekend.

"My cousin Gerard will be there. He's the one member of my family I have anything in common with."

Lois raises her eyebrows.

"We both like seashells and hot chocolate," Elsa answers.

Lois looks at her in surprise, as if to say, *That's all?* Then she smiles, genuinely. "Yes, your party sounds fun. It's strange, I think I've only ever seen you at work."

Elsa replies slowly. "I've been something of a social leper ever since I . . . started working here." She moves her corn around her plate. "I'm tired of it."

Lois thoroughly enjoys a bite of her tuna salad before saying, "Well, it happens to everyone who works for the monster, sooner or later."

"But not you. You go and do fun things on the weekends, don't you? And you've been working here for as long as I can remember."

"But I work for the building, not for him, and there's never any work for a switchboard operator to take home. Besides." She smiles. "I don't let things bother me. I let other people's problems get tangled in my hair during the day and then preen them out at night so I can sleep."

"I could try that," sighs Elsa, "but then I still have all these other things to worry about which *are* my problems." She takes a bite of her roll.

"Such as?"

She feels too embarrassed to tell her coworker about the ongoing gang attacks in her neighborhood, which for starters isn't the safest, but which is the best she can do under her present financial circumstances. The fact that the area is so unsafe is probably the only thing stopping her building association from kicking her out; prospective tenants are thin on the ground. She doesn't want to mention her crumbled relationships with her parents and sister, that they lost their patience and renounced their hopes for her when she didn't evolve into something greater than herself by the time she reached adulthood. She'd in fact rather not acknowledge to Lois her Plainness at all. Likewise her fear that she'll never be better than what she is, and that the world will never forgive her for it.

Lois contemplates Elsa's face while she chews, then asks, "Why are you still in the cubicle maze, anyway? Haven't you been working here for years?"

Elsa knows why she hasn't ever been promoted: her boss is no better than the rest of the world. And although she's worked her tail off her whole time she's been here, he still refuses to see her work as equal to that of a fully realized person. But Elsa keeps silent, staring into her food, chewing ever so thoughtfully.

"Hmm," says Lois, her orange eyes almost narrowing behind her glasses. She looks back down at her plate and then up again with a smile. "So, what time shall we get together?"

6

LOIS ARRIVES first. Elsa is still buckling her shoes when the doorbell rings. She hops to the door, nearly tripping over the hem of her long green skirt. She checks her face in the mirror in the hall, noticing for the first time a large crack in the bottom half of the glass. She pushes her hair out of her eyes and opens the door.

"Hi," says Lois. She looks calm.

"Hi." They just stare at each other a moment, until Elsa remembers to move out of the doorway. Lois walks in and looks around the apartment, taking in the blue and green tones of the walls and old furniture. There are photographs of a younger Elsa here and there, posed with people she doesn't really see anymore. An antique snorkel collecting dust on the mantelpiece, a nautilus drawing taped to one wall—both things she found years ago in a thrift store and bought because they reminded her of Gerard when he was off swimming in the Olympic Development Program. Jonas walks right up to Lois and curls, purring, around her legs.

"Hello," she coos, picking the cat up and nuzzling him.

Elsa stares. "That's Jonas," she says.

"He's sweet." Lois rubs her face against his; it looks for a moment like Jonas's whiskers are poking out of Lois's cheeks. Elsa has never heard such loud purring.

"Do you want him?"

A strange silence as Lois seems to evaluate whether this is a joke. She lets the cat down but he doesn't run away.

Elsa says, "Make yourself at home. I just need to finish my hair," and wanders off to her bedroom.

"Take out your barrette," says Lois, following her. "I've never seen your hair down before." Reluctantly Elsa does; her hair is a mass of tangles falling, falling. "It's so long! I had no idea."

"It's constantly snarled, too. Even after I wash it, I can't get a brush through it." She thinks of the way Joan's hair used to tangle after her swim lessons when they were children, and the way she howled when their mother would yank the knots free with a paddle brush. Frightened by this ritual, Elsa refused to take lessons herself, but now her hair tangles that way, too. "It's like I've always just gotten out of the pool." She looks at Lois's smooth copper curls. "I've tried keeping it short, but it grows so fast I'd be at the salon every three weeks just keeping it above my shoulders." And salons are too expensive to frequent that often on her salary. Elsa has tried cutting it herself, but she can't ever get it even and doesn't know how to cut layers into it to "work with" its texture.

"No wonder you keep it clipped up." Lois touches the dark tangles. "What color is this?" she asks quietly.

"I don't color it. It's always been this way. Strange, too, because my mother and sister are strawberry blondes."

"It shines like the moon on the ocean." Lois gently bats the ends of the tuft she's been playing with.

"It's my one unusual feature, and I have to hide it because it's so messy."

Lois just looks at her, as if she barely understands. She digs a large-tooth wooden comb out of her purse and begins coaxing the ends of Elsa's hair. Some of the tangles give way to recognizable curls, but when she stops combing, the hair seizes back into its former mess. Elsa sighs. Lois seems genuinely confused.

"Don't worry about it," Elsa says. "I'm used to it." She puts her hair back up.

Dinner is pleasant. Lois seems very interested in Gerard's job at the aquarium, which he discusses with candor while keeping a wary eye on Jonas, who seems to be trying to smell him from the comfort of Lois's lap all evening. When Lois excuses herself to use the bathroom, he says quietly, "I understand what you mean about that cat. Maybe Lois will take him home with her."

Then sirens blare down the street and they hear the sound of glass breaking at a distance.

"And perhaps you can get a nice Doberman," he adds.

Over dessert, Elsa mentions her parents have put in a new swimming pool.

"A chlorinated one?" Gerard asks, wrinkling his nose. "So harsh on the skin and hair."

Elsa invites them both to her parents' pool party. Lois's smile fades. "That sounds very nice. But I don't swim."

"Oh, well, you don't have to swim. I don't. Just come with me, and um, enjoy the festivities."

"It would be nice just to sit in the sun for a while." She clears her throat. "My sister drowned in a river when we were young, and I've never been much for water. Swim parties really aren't my thing." Quickly she adds, "But I'll go to keep you company. I'm great at lounging *by* the pool."

Elsa doesn't know how to respond. She can say she's sorry about Lois's sister, but that feels so typical. What surprises her most is that someone has shared something dramatic and personal with her. Even beyond that, the woman's life doesn't seem to have been ruined, only affected, by the event. But then she realizes that if Joan drowned in a river, she might not get all weepy, either.

Gerard asks, "Were you there when it happened?"

The orange eyes look a little distant for half a second, then the dark copper curls bob up and down yes.

"I'm really sorry."

"Thank you."

They nibble in silence until Lois says, "It didn't seem like a scary place at first. We'd heard it was a popular vacation spot. The river had formed almost spontaneously, centuries ago, in the middle of a forest. It didn't look too big, maybe a hundred feet across, but it was mean." She speaks slowly. "Some people we knew from school called it a 'silent killer' because you could never see any movements or hear any disturbances on the surface of the water, but the undercurrents were fierce. And in the rainy season, it could get as deep as twenty feet in some pockets. People would go out there to fish—there was great fishing there, they said. . .”

Elsa knows this place; it's only a couple of hours away. Her stomach turns inexplicably.

“. . . and they'd slip and fall under the water, be carried out by the undertow. They never came back, not alive. The river just sort of took up space until you got close, and then it started killing people. It wasn't surprising to hear of at least four people a summer dying.” She clears her throat. “At least it's a peaceful death. Supposedly the senses dull, like being wrapped in cotton.” She shrugs, affecting nonchalance, but Elsa knows this is probably an act. “I hear it doesn't hurt at all.”

Elsa has been to this river before. Close to a small salt dome in the hill country, it's the only salt-water river for thousands of miles, and this makes it something of a tourist novelty. Her roommates in college took her there one weekend for a camping trip; she was coming into the realization that she might be a Plain One and feeling depressed about it, and they thought she might enjoy getting out of town for a while. Being with them was nice, but the notorious river gave her nightmares and so they cut their weekend short. After graduation, those friends moved away to other cities, and Elsa doesn't talk to them anymore. "Why'd your sister go in?"

"We didn't know any better. It was right after we'd moved from Europe."

Elsa almost jumps for joy at the subject change. "I didn't know you lived in Europe! Where?"

Lois smiles softly, understanding. "All over, really. Would you like to hear about it?"

Elsa would. They don't talk about the river again.

Eventually Lois stands up to leave, and the evening ends. At the door, Gerard has to shove a cloying Jonas away with his foot rather more forcefully than the cat likes. As he leaves, he reminds Elsa to lock all her doors and windows—or perhaps she'd like to stay at his house for a few days?

"No, thanks, I'll be fine here."

Reluctantly, he walks to his car and drives away.

7

THE DAY of the pool party, Elsa puts her charming new swimsuit on underneath her sundress, the one with the starfish on it, hoping she can just sit on a chaise and not have to get into the water. She grabs her sunglasses and a straw hat she found in her closet and rushes excitedly out of her apartment to go pick up Lois, narrowly avoiding closing Jonas's tail in the door as she runs out. Since the night Gerard and Lois came over for dinner, she's begun to anticipate the party with something that isn't dread.

Lois is just coming downstairs from her elevated front porch as Elsa arrives. They smile and wave at each other. Lois looks back at her front window, where a large orange cat perches anxiously on the windowsill. Elsa thinks she sees the cat wave at Lois as she blows it a kiss goodbye. A puddle of rainwater has collected on the cement steps, and turning back to leave, Lois tiptoes to avoid it, but in one unfortunate second she misses a step and trips the rest of the way down to the sidewalk. As

Elsa runs to her, she notices the cat scratch at the window glass and then dart down from the sill. Lois doesn't appear to be hurt at first, just a little shaken.

"Are you all right? I'm so sorry!"

"I'm okay, and it wasn't your fault." But she does let Elsa help her to her feet and brush her hair from her face. The first step she tries to take, she falls again, leaning heavily on Elsa.

"Your ankle! It's already swelling."

There's no question in Elsa's mind: she'll ditch the party in favor of the emergency room.

Lois's injury isn't serious, but the clinic isn't busy, so they leave within a couple of hours. Elsa doesn't have the heart to subject her friend to her family now and thinks she sees relief in Lois's face when she insists on taking her back home.

"You have to make an appearance, you know," she says, gently, when Elsa lingers around the living room after Lois has been comfortably installed on her couch. Her cat hisses at Elsa; Lois hisses at her cat, and the animal scampers away. "I'll be fine here."

So Elsa finds her resolve and drives to her parents' house. Unfortunately, as soon as she gets to the front door, that resolve disintegrates, intimidated by just how wide a gulf lies between everyone's expectations of her and her failure to reach them.

Joan is waiting at the door, Stuart in her arms, when Elsa walks up.

"Where have you been?" she nearly hisses, towering over her younger sister. "People keep asking about you, saying things like they thought Mom and Dad had *two* kids."

"I had to take a friend——"

"This was important to Mom. You should have been on time."

She tries to take this in stride and reaches casually for her nephew. "I'm here now, Joan." But Joan clomps away and hands Stuart off to Neil, who disappears, so adept at staying out of these little conflicts. The harsh reception surprises her; she turns to find her parents standing behind her.

"Elsa, so nice of you to join us," her mother says, bending down to give her a shallow hug as a few guests pass through the hall.

"Sorry I'm late, Mother. My friend twisted——"

"Hello, Elsa," interrupts her father, rocks in his voice. He also hugs her, with one arm, a scotch in his other hand, before nodding and walking off to speak with some other people. Her mother looks at her a moment as if she wants to smile but can't for her disappointment, then follows his example.

Elsa hasn't been close to her parents since her stubbornly Plain adolescence, but she thought they might be less cold toward her in front of guests. She grabs a glass of wine from a nearby tray, then drinks it slowly as she wends her way through the crowd, avoiding her family's narrow looks.

Gerard hasn't come, after all.

There's a new painting in the hallway of a majestic bird ascending from out of a fire. The color palette feels ominous. Violent reds and oranges. The landscape a burnt, ashy desolation. And the bird? More defiance and vengeance than triumph. But the message is clear: *animals transcend whatever struggle you're having.* Another stack of old books on an end table in the corner mars the magazine-quality aesthetic of the room. Elsa looks through the titles, all of them about birds in literature and art. Has her father picked up a new hobby? There must be nine or ten books here. Maybe a new obsession?

A party guest bumps into her from behind, making her upset the stack. The guest hardly seems to notice until Elsa says loudly, "excuse me," and then several people turn to look at her. No one speaks to her, though.

Ah, see, Elsa thinks, smiling awkwardly at these people she doesn't know until she makes it to the backyard, *the Plain daughter has arrived. Has she grown antennae and a tail since we last inspected her? No? What must her parents have done wrong to end up with a daughter like that?* But after she wanders for a few minutes through the outdoor portion of the party, the guests begin to ignore her. She can't entirely blend into the scenery, though, since she's the only one wearing more than a bathing suit. Elsa removes her sundress and puts it on the back of a chaise.

The afternoon is still very warm, and soon nearly everyone who was on the patio has climbed into the large pool. Neil comes outside, still holding Stuart, and Elsa beckons them over. Neil sits down on a chair next to her, and when she holds her arms out for the baby, he hands him over.

"How've you been?" she asks, hoping he'll engage in small talk at least.

"You know, same as always," he says, running his pointed fingernails through his silky black hair. The tip of his long, sharp nose points downward when he speaks. "Stuart is already running—"

Angélique Jamail

"So soon?" Elsa asks, admiring her nephew as he excitedly claps his hands together and squeals. "Well, I suppose Joan was an early walker, too."

Neil nods. "It's hard to keep up with him these days. He gets into stuff a lot."

"That must be exhausting." Neil nods again. *Maybe that's why Joan is so rude all the time,* Elsa thinks. *She's tired.* Aloud, she says, "Well, he's a sweet baby, regardless."

"Thanks." Neil smiles. "So, how've you been lately?"

Where to begin? Elsa doesn't really want to catalog her woes to her brother-in-law. Even though he has always been polite to her, she knows he doesn't really want to hear about them. So she shrugs. "You know, same as always."

He nods a third time. They sit quietly for a couple more minutes, focusing on Stuart's clever little sounds and his apparent fascination with a lizard that has climbed up the back of his father's chair. He coos at it. No doubt he'll be talking soon.

Neil stifles a yawn and runs a hand over his golden eyes. His shoulders slump. Elsa can see how tired he is.

"You know," she says, "if you'd like, I could maybe babysit some time." She can figure out a way around her work schedule.

"That's nice of you. Thanks for the offer," Neil says. "I'll talk to Joan about it."

Elsa continues, "I noticed you'd brought over some more books for my dad. Are they related to your research?" Neil is a literature professor and always has some deeply cerebral project percolating in the background.

"They are," he says, eyes on Stuart, one hand poised to catch him if he teeters too far off Elsa's lap. "Bird signs."

"What are those?" She already has a vague idea but just wants him to keep talking to her.

"Omens, like in classical stories. The ancient Greeks in particular thought the movements of birds heralded the future, that they could predict outcomes from things like the direction an eagle was flying overhead at a particularly momentous—"

A crow caw, loud and urgent, shrieks through the party. Several guests startle; one drops his drink. They look around to see who has made the noise. The upper branches of a tree in the next-door neighbor's yard rustle.

Neil sighs. "Like that."

"What does it mean?" she asks.

Just then Joan bursts through the back door, a frantic look in her eyes. "There you are!" she says when her eyes land on Elsa.

"Yes?" Elsa asks, surprised that Joan might be looking for her.

Joan walks briskly over and retrieves her son from Elsa's lap without a word. Then she turns to Neil. "Mom wants a family picture in the pool."

"Okay," he sighs again. "Let's get Stuart changed." They walk inside without even a glance back at Elsa, who is left to wonder whether she should also get into the pool or just leave now.

A moment later the photographer comes outside, Elsa's parents and Joan's little family in tow. There's much cheerful hubbub as they all decide on the best spot to pose everyone. Their jolly, tipsy guests clear a shady spot near the stone waterfall. Elsa watches from the chaise until her whole family is posed, and then the photographer asks, "Don't you have another daughter?"

Elsa's father lands his stony gaze upon her and points. "Aren't you going to join us," he says. It doesn't sound like a question.

Elsa stands and walks slowly over. She doesn't want to get in the water. "Can I just sit on the rocks here at the back?" she asks.

"No, the composition will be off," the photographer says.

"Get in the water, Elsa," her mother insists.

She takes a deep breath, steels her nerves, and slips into the pool. The water is cold here in the shade, and the stinging pain she braced herself for doesn't come. She begins to relax a little, and they take several photos. Then her family scatters, leaving Elsa alone. A few other guests are in and out of the water, but they leave her alone, too. Surprisingly, the sensation of being wet actually feels refreshing under the hot sun. She half jumps, half floats around in the shallow end for a while until the noise of the party guests, laughing, sipping cocktails, splashing each other, rings in her ears like an alarm.

Elsa is lost in a gaggle of people who do not care about her. As she acclimates to the temperature of the water, its soothing coolness disappears. After a few minutes, her limbs start to burn. She hurries to the steps to sit and look at her skin.

Her legs have broken out in some sort of rash, her skin now splotched and stinging, and in some places, already peeling. Is the chlorine just too strong? But it doesn't seem to be bothering anyone else. Scared, she trips up the steps and across the deck to grab a towel from a nearby chair. When she pulls the towel away, there's blood on it.

"Hey, that's my towel!" An angry guest points his drink at her and hollers when he sees her blood. "What have you *done*?"

Other guests stare. Elsa looks down and sees red-streaked legs, flaking skin. Nauseated, she runs quickly to the downstairs powder room and locks herself in. The people's voices on the other side of the door are loud and garbled.

Before her stomach stops turning, her father knocks. "Elsa," he says, "your mother wants you to leave."

What? Each time she touches her legs, tiny rivulets of blood drip, flakes of her flesh cascading onto the beige travertine floor.

"Go home, get cleaned up. Call us next week. Or not."

No . . . oh God, my legs . . .

"Can you hear me in there? She says you've ruined her party."

Elsa can barely breathe. Her father's footsteps march briskly away. It takes a while for her to calm down, for the bleeding to stop. She stays in the bathroom so long it becomes inconvenient to the other guests. When she does emerge, she hurries past their stares to retrieve her sundress and then leaves without telling anyone goodbye.

Elsa cries over her stinging legs and her family and her plain, Plain life the whole way home.

On a high bridge a mile from her apartment, an unexpected flock of pigeons seems to be holding a haughty conference in the roadway. Elsa slows down to avoid scattering them, but then a convertible speeds up behind her, horn honking. Her jalopy can't move out of its way fast enough, and the other car crops close, jostling her up onto the curb. The pigeons fly off angrily, a few feathers landing on her windshield. She bangs to a stop on the small shoulder next to the guardrail.

Wolfish menace glares in the other driver's eyes as he sneers at her.

"What's wrong with everyone?" she screams, fumbling herself out of the car. "You could've killed me!" she shrieks at the other driver, whose car is already howling off. Slowly Elsa's sobs stop, and she realizes that if she'd had a bigger car, the guardrail couldn't have

stopped it. "I almost died," she whispers, imagining herself flying off the overpass with the other birds, arcing through space to a fiery conclusion, the grief of her troubles incinerating in a purifying conflagration. The thought of such an outcome distracts her from her disastrous day, and here in the twilit silence of an empty road, she begins to feel peaceful—or at least calm enough to climb back in, shift her car back onto the street, and drive slowly home.

The thought of never seeing her family again, or trudging at her job, or being made to feel *less than* because she doesn't live up to the world's expectations, because she's just the person she is and nothing more . . . these are things she'd rather live without.

But they are all, inextricably, the sinews of her life.

8

AS ELSA leaves her apartment the next Friday, scrawled red graffiti on the fence across the street catches her eye. *Plaine Onez*, it says, *yor dayz arr numbrred.* Not the most eloquent or original text, but the messy letters make their point.

Elsa has barely been keeping the wolves at bay. Another threat-of-eviction notice is nailed to her door. When she arrives at work, Lois hands her a message from Gerard, saying he will be picking her up that afternoon and to wait for him at her office.

He takes her to dinner and tells her, "I think you should stay at my house a while. The guest room is all set up for you."

"Why?"

"Riots. Wolves. I've been watching the news. I'm worried about you."

She consents to just the weekend—any longer than that, and hungry Jonas might kill her in her sleep when she gets back. She can see her cousin isn't entirely satisfied, but pushiness isn't his style.

When Gerard takes her home after dinner to collect a few things and leave out food for Jonas, her mailbox has been set on fire and her apartment broken into. Nothing much taken, but the place has been vandalized, the locks on her door busted.

"This place isn't safe."

Through the pinprick numbness of Elsa's anxiety, she isn't certain which of them has said it, but she knows that's how she feels. She doesn't talk on the way to his house.

The next morning Elsa wakes from a dream in which she has fallen into Gerard's pool. He's waiting for her under the water, his spiky brown hair looking more ridged than ever. The pool is larger than life, the kelp he's planted in it stretching into a forest. She can feel the sunlight streaming down through the water, and it warms her skin. She hangs suspended beneath the surface, the sun penetrating until she burns. Her cousin looks dispassionately on as she dissolves into ash and dissipates into the current, becoming the sunlight itself. Disembodied, Elsa watches Gerard from above the pool as he slips back and swims away.

When she wakes, she hears splashing and walks from her bed to the open window. He's down there in the backyard, conducting his water exercises. Elsa dresses and goes downstairs to the kitchen. *Some saltines will settle my stomach,* she thinks, still worried about the break-in, and pokes around in the cabinets until she finds some, then takes a handful into Gerard's study, where she knows she can browse the newspaper. One unusual article catches her eye, about a phoenix. She carries it outside to the pool and tells him about it.

"Do you think this is real?" she asks, keeping her distance from the water's edge.

"I don't know," he shrugs, water dripping from the end of his long, blunt nose. "There hasn't been a phoenix in so many generations. It could be a hoax."

"Wouldn't that be something?" she asks thoughtfully, imagining the glorious fiery feathers, the golden splendor.

"It sounds awful. Just think of the trauma that precedes that kind of transformation. It's a good thing we only get one at a time, if that."

She doesn't have a response for that.

"Come swimming," he says. "The water's great."

The dream lingers at the back of her mind. In it, she didn't feel pain, but this is real life, and she doesn't want to repeat the experience she had at her parents' house. "No, thank you," she snaps, her mental image blurred. "You weren't at the last pool party I went to."

He sighs. "You mean your parents' shindig?" He shakes his head. "What happened?"

She wants to explain about the stinging and the blood and the aggressive other driver on her way home, but she doesn't think Gerard will understand her, and that thought is too painful. She feels suddenly even more alone in the world. "Why didn't you come?"

He raises his eyebrows. "Chlorine, Elsa? What did you expect?"

She doesn't want to talk about that anymore and turns her attention back to the folded newspaper in her hand. She scans the article again for any hint of its veracity. "Have you seen anything else about this?" she asks, waving it at him.

"Nope. Tricky—and time-consuming—to verify." He glides backward through the water, sleekly hypnotic as the waves rise up around his shoulders. "Problem is, a phoenix isn't born that way. Puberty doesn't bring it out."

The triumphant avian resurrecting from a life of ash and despair. The gravitas after a life of Plainness. "Right. You'd have to die first."

44

Gerard nods and dunks to turn another flip.

Proving them all wrong.

When he resurfaces, he splashes water playfully at Elsa. The water soaks the article, rendering it nearly unreadable, and she scowls at him as he chuckles, annoyed enough that she doesn't even notice at first that the water he splashed onto her skirt has also hit her bare feet. She's back inside changing clothes when she sees the drops glistening on her skin.

Elsa tenderly touches her feet, imagines sharp talons at the ends of her toes, painted gold and red. She turns back to the soggy newspaper. A blurb at the end of the article lists the crime statistics for their city, arranged by neighborhood. The stats make it sound like she's living in a war zone. The wolves are growing bolder.

A phoenix could transcend all of that, though. The incredible power, the resurrection into something so much greater than the Plainness you started from. Wolves don't seem to respect or be afraid of anything, but they would probably bend before a firebird.

The trilling sounds of pine warblers and cardinals sound lovely to Elsa's ears. A blackbird in the tree outside her open window flashes iridescent feathers. It takes off from its branch, gracefully sweeping through the sky in a stunning display of sovereignty.

Angélique Jamail

Elsa thinks it would be nice to be a bird.

9

A‍T WORK the next week a clerk in a cubicle close to Elsa's shrieks. Several people, including Elsa and Lois, pop around to see what's the matter. The woman, easily forty years old, is staring at her arms in disbelief, turning them over and over, gingerly fondling the tiny feathers poking up from her skin—feathers that weren't there the day before.

The woman's small audience murmurs approval and even relief as her eyes well up with joyful tears.

"How nice for her," Elsa says flatly.

Lois looks thoughtfully at the woman, and then at Elsa. "I'm hungry," she says. "Let's go get a snack."

As they begin to leave, the monster's door opens and his voice booms from within, "Elsa, get your mediocre ass in here *now*."

She and Lois look at each other; Elsa sees her own fear reflected in Lois's eyes. She walks numbly inside and the door slams behind her.

The dreaded boss behind the big oak desk is pacing, snorting in anger. The room is too warm, the walls too close.

"I am dissatisfied with your work," he says, his voice rumbling low with menace. This is the first time he's expressed disapproval of her *work* since she took this job, so many years ago she barely remembers when it was. He suddenly leans hard across his desk, a threatening snarl distorting his lips. She refuses to flinch.

"Do you imagine that, just because you work so many hours, you are exempt from my standards?" he growls. "*Underling.* Being a Plain One does not increase your esteem in my eyes."

Finally, he has deigned to speak her one weakness, the only thing she can't make better by working harder.

"I'd thought you might make manager one day," he sneers. "But unless something very dramatic happens, you'll remain a peon for the rest of your life."

For the rest of your life . . . The words echo in her mind as he stomps back and forth behind his enormous desk. Her stomach roils.

He snatches up a stack of papers and waves it at her. "Did you even proofread the reports you turned in this week?" He roars in frustration; her ears ring. "You have no concept of hard work."

How can you say that? she wants to scream. *You have no concept of—of anything! You know nothing about my life! Nothing of value.* But she knows to keep silent.

He peers at her from across his desk. "Do you want to say something?" he bellows. She shakes her head. *"Good."* He throws the papers at her. "Turn in another shitty assignment, and it'll be your last." His eyes, murderous, glower at her. In a low voice, he says, "No one out there will miss you."

She keeps her tears at bay and just manages to breathe slowly enough to walk away when he tells her to get out.

She knows one thing for certain as she walks back to her desk, her coworkers' eyes all boring into her shame. She will not remain at this job much longer.

She sits, and Lois, who has been waiting for Elsa in her cubicle, puts a condoling arm around her. Her touch is kind, but Elsa can see no optimism in those lovely orange eyes.

Elsa ignores her briefcase on her desk when she leaves. As she exits the building, exotic birds perch upon the patio tables by the doors. She gazes at their glossy feathers, imagines how silky they feel. Their noble beaks

Angélique Jamail

and festive coxcombs seem to incline toward her as she passes.

She feels suddenly numb, the sounds of the plaza and the street beyond dampening in her ears, as if she were wrapped in cotton. The image of the river meanders its way into her mind.

Elsa smiles in grim relief on the way home at the thought of dissolving all her problems, drowning them in an apathetic bath.

10

ELSA STARES, hypnotized by the quiet, determined river. It seems peaceful enough on this bank to have a picnic, but she hears Lois's words echoing in her head: ". . . trapped under the surface in a swift water current . . . no one would ever know . . . silent killer." How dramatic that phrase, and how hopeful she now feels. Lois's voice echoes again: "a peaceful death." But this won't really be dying, of course. It will be rebirth. Metamorphosis. If it works. But it has to work—what other choice does she have? Wolves? The monster? Something has to give, and this path offers her a chance, rather than pain and mutilation.

She put a letter in the mail to Neil with a single sentence written on it: *Tell my father I saw the signs, and I tried.* If anyone will understand that, it's Neil. And if he doesn't, fine. That's out of her hands.

She hasn't said anything to Gerard, not wanting him to try to talk her out of it. She recognizes the oddity of a phoenix rising from a river, but for the first time she can remember, the water beckons her instinctively. *Maybe that's because of Gerard,* she thinks, remembering her dream.

She wonders what will happen, whether she'll emerge a fine, fiery bird—or if not, how long it'll take for people to find and identify her. *Either way, these problems are over.*

She steps out of her shoes and walks over the roots of giant trees down to the water's edge. The shade of branches overhead makes everything darker than she would've thought; she can't see past the skim surface. That doesn't stop her staring, though, as if trying to see the currents themselves, even as she mechanically unbuttons her dress down to her hips. She shrugs one side at a time until the fabric slides to the ground, then walks out of the pile and into the water in her underwear.

Cold. Her nerves almost retreat, eyes closed and sharp intake of breath. She tenses for the pain, but the briny water is so cold it doesn't come. Soon she opens up and begins to unclench to the new sensation of wet. Wades in up to her thighs and stops again. The water feels warmer now, but it still isn't prickling. *This must be the right course, then,* she thinks, and an unfamiliar yet welcome . . . peace? Some soothed feeling comes over her. She tries to take in her surroundings: the reticent light under the trees, the deceptive calm of the water, a chorus of birdsong welcoming her. If she listens carefully, she can hear the white noise of a far-off waterfall. The setting is darkly beautiful.

Elsa balls herself up to let the water spin her around and over. As her head slides under the surface, she feels the long tentacles of her hair come loose, cover her face and the front of her body, and finally, an undercurrent rushes past her with such force that it pulls her limbs away from her torso as she's sped downriver.

She tries not to move, not to attempt to swim, just surrenders herself to the river, her eyes steadfastly shut. Screwing up her last bit of courage, she opens her mouth and nose under the water. Gushing drink and kelp-like hair choke her, but she fights the instinct to lift her head above the water, tightly folds her arms behind her back. Presses her legs together and fights the current from tearing them open. She drinks in more of the river, painfully, forcefully.

She expects the edges of her consciousness to fade, but they don't. She gulps again, this time also through her nose, certain this will be her last effort as the river drags her on. The water feels soft like fog, but the currents are getting faster. She must be close to the falls by now, but is dismayed not to find her mental acuity weakening. In fact, she feels . . . fine.

Her arms push the hair from her face; it streams out behind her in long, smooth waves. She doesn't need to swim; the water carries her swiftly. The water doesn't sting her eyes when she opens them. Elsa can see clearly, tree roots and rocks and fish, all calmly disregarding her as well as each other.

This is bizarre, she thinks. *Have I already drowned and not noticed?* But that doesn't seem right, so she drags her head above the water, setting her body more upright. Her feet can't reach the bottom; the current still carries her. She looks over the surface of the water at the ordinary riverbank and trees and knows she's still alive. She blinks water from her eyes and looks around again; embedded in the riverbank, the roots of the trees form a graceful lattice that makes them appear to cradle each other. The rocks shine in the half-light like earthen jewels. The fish seem to dance. Every part of her surroundings is in harmony . . .

Then panic overwhelms her as she sees the falls rapidly approaching. They're steep. The water and rocks at their edge churn a ferocious white, jut a razor-sharp brown. The idea of hitting her head against them no longer seems comforting.

No, *no*, she *doesn't* want to drown, and she wants even less to be broken against the rocks. The instinct to survive floods her body, propelling her flailing limbs to find strength, find purpose.

It's hard, but she can keep her head mostly above water. Her long hair tangles around her, though, disconcertingly whipping against her face as the waves grow rougher. She's too far from the riverbank to reach a handhold, the roots too far away. She tries a frantic dog-paddle toward the water's edge, but her legs won't move apart; they're stuck to each other. She can only flip her feet at the ankles—and in a forceful surge she does, violently, nearly scraping her skin on smaller rocks being carried by the river too, as her arms thrash to pull the lower half of her body out of the current. Just before the falls rush up, she manages to find the riverbank and cling to a root.

But the current is still with her, and soon she's being dragged to the drop-off again. She holds her breath, bracing for the plunge, and catches the flatter side of a rock just before tumbling over the edge.

Water crashes against her, blinding and choking her, but she clings her arms around the sides of the boulder, begging it to bulwark. The current is tearing her from her rock and she gives a little cry of fear, but then she can breathe enough to climb on top. It rises large a couple of feet above the surface, and finally she's sitting on it, still holding desperately on, sobbing.

She peels her legs apart, amazed and confused by the harsh stickiness of her flesh. But this is a mystery for another moment, one in which she isn't stranded, mostly naked, in the middle of a treacherous river.

Elsa looks for a way out of her mess. Maybe she can climb from her rock over to another and another until she reaches the riverbank and can climb up onto it? She can't swim back to her clothing against such fast-moving water and doesn't relish walking through the woods in soaking underclothes.

But that's what I get for trying to drown myself, she thinks bitterly. *Who the hell do I think I am, anyway? This isn't Shakespeare.*

The anger prompts her resolve, and she begins boulder hopping. At first, it seems like her legs won't work very well, but she regains her balance and soon reaches the bank.

She'll go home, maybe find another job, if she can. Maybe find another city. She'll miss Gerard, and Lois, but they'll keep in touch. One thing is certain, though: she's done with this miserable nonsense.

Elsa hurries back as well as she can in the predictably freezing air. At least it isn't completely dark yet. A couple of times she cuts her feet, tripping over stones and tree roots, but eventually she finds her dress and puts it back on. She cleans her feet as best she can at the water's edge and gingerly puts on her shoes.

The journey back to town and her apartment is resigned; on the way, she remembers that, logistically, a Plain One would have the same difficulties everywhere, and her exhaustion takes some of the steam out of her plan to forge a new life.

"Phoenix, ha. What makes you so special?" she mutters angrily to herself as she drives. "Committing suicide?" She snorts in exasperation.

I couldn't even do that right.

She doesn't have the energy to think of a real solution.

11

BEFORE GOING to the river, Elsa left Lois a message. Had she spoken to her directly, she might not have felt the determination she needed to go. Jonas tried repeatedly to bite Elsa's hand as she dialed the number.

"Quit it, Jonas, I need to make this call." That hadn't worked. "Jonas, relax! I'm trying to make provisions for you to be fed and nurtured after I'm gone."

Who was she kidding? She no longer cared beyond idle curiosity what happened to him.

He wrapped his claws around her wrist and took a large bite of her hand. She shrieked with pain and pushed the cat roughly away. "Fine! You can *starve!*"

But she had more important things to tell than anything about Jonas, and so she closed herself up in the bathroom to make the call. Then, as she dialed Lois's number, every meaningful thing she wanted to say got lodged in her throat like a chicken bone. It took a couple of tries to complete the call. Finally, she spoke a message into Lois's answering machine: "It's Elsa. I'm going to the river and won't be back to work. *If* you're so inclined, please feed my ass of a cat. The little mongrel won't stop biting me. Door'll be unlocked." She paused before adding gently, "Thank you." Elsa felt she was thanking her for so many things.

For being her friend. For caring what happened to her. For living so doggedly and authentically and unapologetically as her self.

For inspiring Elsa, even if she hadn't succeeded in following Lois's example. But Elsa couldn't say any of that out loud. The river would do it for her.

Would've done it for her. Hadn't done much for her.

Now, Elsa trudges up the steps to her apartment. She isn't wet anymore, except for the thicker parts of her hair, which are still damp. Her clothes have mostly dried, although a tell-tale musty odor will reveal where her wet underclothes striped the driver's seat through her dress.

She pauses with her hand on the doorknob, reading an actual eviction notice. The building association has given her one month. She leans her head against the door and knocks against it with her forehead a couple of times.

She hasn't been gone even a day, but already the place feels unfamiliar. Hopefully, Lois won't have gotten the message yet, and Elsa can leave another one saying it was all a dream, all a joke, all useless, but she *would* like some company.

She walks through the door and into her kitchen. Jonas is eating and takes no notice of her. She closes the door and looks into the hallway; a single light shines, from her bedroom. She walks toward it and finds Lois reading, propped up by the pillows of Elsa's bed, by the lamp on the nightstand.

"Hi," says Lois. Elsa doesn't know what to reply. Did the copper-haired woman not interpret her message accurately? "How are you?"

Elsa finds her voice. "You seem nonchalant."

"I didn't expect you would drown."

"Why not?"

Lois shrugs. She pats the bed next to her. Elsa climbs up onto it and stretches herself out from her shoulders to her toes, her legs and feet together as they were in the water, then buries her face into Lois's shoulder and weeps while Lois pats her hand gently, an arm around her.

The last time Elsa felt so comforted was when she broke her arm in the fourth grade and her mother sat up with her all night while she got used to her new cast. In her exhaustion, Elsa admits to herself that in the disappointment her adulthood has turned out to be, she has missed this love most of all.

12

ELSA NEVER knows how long they stay that way before she falls asleep, but when the sunlight of the next day wakes her, Lois is curled into an oval. Jonas sleeps peacefully in a chair across from the bed. Elsa stretches, and Lois opens her eyes.

"Good morning," she says, dark copper curls everywhere. She sits up and shifts her wrinkled clothes, pats them down repeatedly. She arches her back, stretches her legs until her ankles pop. She rubs the side of her nose with the back of her thumb.

"Good morning," Elsa says. She stands up from the bed and looks down at herself. "I'm gross."

"Not at all. You smell lovely." This seems funny and they laugh. "I'll fix you a bath."

Elsa is about to protest but then thinks better of it. Maybe if the river didn't burn her, the bath won't, either. And she feels rank. Lois looks so earnest, so helpful. It's at least worth trying.

"How do you feel?"

Elsa thinks for a moment. "Better." She thinks some more. "Different."

"Maybe you're just relaxed," says Lois. "You slept a long time, solidly. The alarm clock didn't even wake you."

"I must've forgotten to turn it off before I left yesterday." Elsa looks at the time: half past nine. "We're *really* late for work." She feels a nervous twinge.

"Do you want to call in?" asks Lois.

"Yes. Not really. Maybe." They both smile. "I'll think about it while I'm in the tub."

Lois walks out of the room and down the hallway into the kitchen. Elsa watches her from the doorway. Her friend looks around in the cabinets until she finds a box of sea salt.

"What's that for?"

"It draws a wonderful bath. You'll like it." Lois disappears into the bathroom and Elsa can hear the creaky gush of water from the faucet; the bath spout seems not to know what to make of its new usefulness. When it's time for her to go in, the water looks inviting in a way the cold river, its overwhelming largeness towered over by the darkest canopy of trees, simply didn't. "See you, then," says Lois, exiting the bathroom.

"Are you leaving?"

"No, no, I'm just going to make some toast." She smiles as she closes the door behind her.

Elsa sheds her clothes onto the floor and steps into the tub. It's smaller than she remembers, but the warm water . . . incredibly . . . feels . . . soothing. She sinks slowly into it and stretches her legs out, leans her head back onto the ledge behind her. There are shells along the edge of the tub that she collected from shops along the boardwalk when she was in college. She's forgotten about them, though they've always been there, hiding among the shampoo and soaps. One of them is a small conch. She picks it up and turns it over in her hands, feeling its beautiful ridges and curves and the smooth, marble-like inside. She closes her eyes and enjoys the simple act of stretching her legs and feet and toes as far as they will go. She holds the tension in her muscles for a long time.

When they start to feel uncomfortable, she still doesn't let go. The salty water seems to eddy around her limbs but she doesn't move, she just lies back, lies still. She doesn't open her eyes again until she feels a stickiness at her knees that prevents her from pulling them apart, and when she does finally look down, her legs are no longer there.

In their place is a fishtail.

Elsa just stares at herself for several minutes. When she has gotten used to the idea, she feels an enormous grin spread over her face. She flips her fins—those were toes when she woke up this morning!—until she's splashing water onto the bathroom floor.

"Is everything working out in there?" calls Lois from the other side of the door.

"Yes!" Elsa startles herself with her own enthusiasm. "Yes, it's—it's fine. Just fine." She looks down at herself, at the curves of her breasts and the graceful slope of her stomach easing into the newly darkened flesh of her fin. At her hair, nearly blue in its blackness, the customary tangles soothed away in the water, the long, wet tufts draped across the geography of her body. She adds quietly, "It's amazing." After another minute, she calls out, "Would you like to go to the beach today?"

There's a pause from the other room. "Elsa. Do you want me to call the office?"

She thinks for a moment, then says, "I'll call in. And I'll tell them I'm not coming back, ever."

"No problem." She can hear Lois smiling. Just beyond the door, Jonas meows, insistent, then begins purring and scratching frantically at the door. Lois hushes him and lures him away with some food.

Elsa looks around the room with fresh, cheerful eyes. Everything will be different now; she can feel it in every cell of her new body. She'll no longer have to leave the "Animal Affinity" section of an employment application blank, and with all the numerous jobs she's had to perform for the monster on her resumé, there won't be many positions she can't get now.

She'll move out of this cramped apartment, too; she can stay with her cousin until she gets settled. He won't mind. She imagines swimming with him, racing across the pool as they raced across the backyard when they were children. And he won't have to worry about her safety anymore, or give her pitying looks when she tells him everything is fine.

Because it will be, and even better than fine. She won't have to hide any part of herself, not anymore. She now has her *self*. Elsa nearly squeals. The inadequacy she's felt for so many years has dissolved into the water of her bath, and she knows that when she drains the tub, that sadness will swirl away, too.

Just then, she notices the phone is still next to the sink where she left it the day before. If she lifts herself up just a little—it isn't so hard to do, after all, her fleshy tail sliding along the porcelain—she can reach it. The movement makes her pause, though: how is she going to get out of the tub? Get around her apartment? Drive to the beach? How long will this initial transformed shape last before she returns to her original—but now enhanced—form?

She has no idea, but she knows who will. She dials Gerard's number, and while she listens to the ringing, she decides that he can tell the rest of their family if he wants to. Her parents' and sister's reactions have no bearing on the calculus of the new life she's going to create.

When he answers, she tells him, "Come over. I have the most wonderful news."

BOOK CLUB
DISCUSSION GUIDE

1. The concept of maturity seems linked to the emergence of one's animal affinity. Does it appear that physical and emotional maturity are linked in this way in the characters' thoughts and actions?

2. Why does Elsa's attempt to unalive herself fail? Consider the philosophical reasons as well as logistical ones.

3. Do you think Gerard and Lois understand something about Elsa that she does not? Do they know what her potential transformation is, or do they just see her value as an individual? When considering their regard for Elsa, how much does it matter what they know or don't know about her?

4. What do you think is next for Elsa, both immediately and in the long term? Should she stay in her town or find another? What would be the consequences of each choice?

5. Are Elsa's problems over, after her transformation? How might they be resolved now? Why might they not be?

6. How should parents treat their children's individuality when their differences seem difficult to handle? What is their role and responsibility, if any? If parents have an obligation to their children's uniqueness, does this obligation go away when the child is an adult?

7. It can be agonizing to be different, especially when you're young, and yet many outstanding individuals were "different" when they were growing up. How can you encourage young people to embrace their authentic selves—rather than just blending in with the crowd? Are there different strategies for different genders? Should there be?

TELL ME, OF THE DEAD

As a writer, I have, on occasion, been accused of pulling my punches.

Not often, but that criticism has been levied once or twice in feedback on a WIP. And like most writers, I've fallen into the hateful trap of obsessing over negative details (valid or not), rather than seeing what actually works in a manuscript. Some might call this counterproductive. Usually they'd be right, but paying careful attention to critiques that stick in my craw has helped me improve my work. And grow a thicker skin.

One time, though, this fixation led to a change in me, not in the manuscript. I was going through final edits of *A Narrowing Path*. In it, a character considers drowning herself. I knew in my gut the end of her arc was the right one. I wasn't trying to be Kate Chopin or Shakespeare; nor was I writing realistic fiction. The Animal Affinities series is arguably magic realism, a fantastical type of literary fiction. I could make *anything* happen to this character that I wanted, John Updike and the laws of nature be damned.

"You want nice things to happen to your characters," a workshop partner once insisted at me, her nose crinkling just slightly above her tooth-bared smile. "You love tidy endings."

When she said it, I didn't roll my eyes.

But while finishing the edits for *A Narrowing Path*, I did wonder if I had a problem.

That week, I got a call from a friend I'd gone to college with, and she had something shocking to tell me. Another of our contemporaries, Heather, whom I hadn't seen in a few years since we'd both ended up at the wedding of another of our classmates, had died. She'd drowned while on vacation with her family. Tethered to a paddleboard in a calm-looking but swiftly moving river, snagged underwater by some fallen tree branches, her board got lodged, and she got held under. Her ten-year-old daughter screamed and screamed for help, but when it arrived, Heather was no longer alive.

Every part of this, from the unnecessary loss of my friend's life to the trauma of her young daughter's watching it happen, is horrifying. There's no getting around that, and no amount of condolences, though appreciated, will ever change a single detail.

In my grief, I put my story away. I couldn't even look at it. But deadlines don't care about the dead, and eventually I had to bring it back up and smooth out those final line edits.

I considered changing the story, but I knew that wouldn't be right for the character. I fixed a comma splice and changed a few more words around. I tweaked a metaphor and added a line of wry dialogue. In places, I'm told, *A Narrowing Path* is funny, but I couldn't feel it anymore. I couldn't take pleasure in the craft of writing. All I could hear was Heather's daughter crying for help, and all I could think about was that the child's anguished shriek was the last thing her mother ever heard.

I'm told that drowning is a peaceful way to go. The senses dull, everything fades into a heavy quiet, a liquid thrumming. Like going to sleep on a boat, maybe like going to sleep in the womb. I don't know, but the idea that there is peace, that one goes back to the beginning of things, was strangely comforting.

I added that detail to the story. That was the extent to which I changed my manuscript as a result of Heather's death.

But the more I worked on those edits, the more I let the story wash over me, the more I submerged myself in it—the more my grief subsided, like ripples on a lake growing wider, gentler until indistinguishable from the lake itself. No longer a disturbance, but a feature of the world. I will never lose this grief. I don't have to. It simply is.

Tim O'Brien, in *The Things They Carried*, speaks of writing as unintentional therapy. I don't think that's what was happening to me, not really, not in the way writing about the Vietnam War probably staved off the worst outcomes of his PTSD. But in the chapter "The Lives of the Dead," he writes about a nine-year-old girl named Linda, whom his character Timmy loved and lost to brain cancer in elementary school. Later, in his adult life, he dreams her back into existence. She speaks of the afterlife as if being dead were like being a book on a shelf that no one is reading at the moment. It's not some agony or paradise, it just *is*. And he realizes that writing a book about a character who is himself is like trying to save his own young life "with a story."

I don't know if something could have saved my friend's life. I don't know whether it's better or worse to think that her accident could have been prevented. I look at my own young children, one of them on the cusp of middle school, and worry pre-emptively about the things they're going to deal with in the world, and I hope that the worst tragedy they ever encounter is the death of our ancient cat. We cannot save everyone, after all.

But we try. We are writers and we destroy lives and worlds and ideologies. And sometimes, we don't.

And sometimes, regardless of what the average cynic might suggest, that choice is the right one.

Angélique Jamail

An earlier version of this essay first appeared on Jennifer Brozek's blog on June 10, 2015.

ACKNOWLEDGEMENTS

In the summer of 1998, after a few years of writing nothing but emails and poetry, I sat down and typed this sentence: "Elsa had several problems, including a challenging family, a difficult boss, and a cat who—she was convinced—wanted to eat her." I then proceeded to write one page of this story every day until I had a draft. I workshopped it, revised it, tucked it into a file for six or seven years to incubate, dug it out again and workshopped and revised it some more, put it away for a couple more years, excavated it and workshopped it again, edited—*lather, rinse, repeat*—until I had, for the most part, this story you've just read. In those years when the story lay dormant, I was busy in the process of changing as a person and as a writer, growing up. And in the ten years since this story's publication, I've grown even more, as a writer and as a person, and the world has changed a lot, too. This new edition, I hope, reflects some of that evolution in the story's fabric and in my telling of it.

A slew of wonderful people supported me on Elsa's journey, as well as on mine as a writer, and I appreciate all of them for their love and encouragement over the years. In particular I want to thank some people who have helped make *A Narrowing Path* a real live book. First, Ynes Freeman and Leo Otherland at Memento Vivere Press, who read *Finis.* and thought my Animal Affinities series was not only something they enjoyed but also something they could help me grow. These fierce champions of my writing have been a dream to work with, and I love the way this series is evolving with their partnership.

The biggest heart emojis in the world go out to Sarah Warburton and David Jón Fuller, my fiction write-or-dies, for the endless conversations about craft and life and for all the chocolate and all the knitting. Seriously, all the chocolate. All the knitting.

In addition to Sarah and David, my Saturday morning writing sprinters Melissa Huckabay and Courtney O'Banion Smith deserve my sincere thanks. How would we ever get anything done without Saturday mornings? And my affectionate appreciation also goes out to my colleagues—Christa, Michael, Evan, Nadine, Jennifer, Scott, Katie, Andy, Olen, Charlie, and Shelia *in particular* among others—who make my already usually pretty great day job so good that I have the mental space and clarity to make my writing job happen. It's uncommon to find true friendship among one's coworkers, and I know how lucky I am to have done so.

And an exceptional thank you to my readers, because without you I'm just scribbling away in a journal. You know I do all of this for you, right? True story.

Finally, I must mention with immense gratitude Aaron, Han, and Liam, without whose patience and love I couldn't possibly engage in the career of writing.

Thank you, thank you all.

ABOUT THE AUTHOR

Angélique Jamail is an award-winning Lebanese-American author whose poetry, essays, and short fiction have appeared in dozens of journals and anthologies and been featured on the radio. The first time she read one of her short stories to an audience was fourth grade; the reaction to it was a character-building experience. Her other books include the poetry collection *The Sharp Edges of Water*, and she's the creator of the zine *Sonic Chihuahua*. She serves on the Board of Directors for Mutabilis Press and is the Director of Creative Writing at The Kinkaid School. She resides in the Houston area with her family and their cats; she has otherwise lived inside her imagination pretty much her whole life.

You can find Angélique Jamail on social media and at her blog, SapphosTorque.com, and she's available for book club appearances in person or via live video.

www.AngeliqueJamail.com